Scotland for us! & besides they hate to send Suff[ragettes] to prison up in the provinces & in Scotland - we are especially sure to get off because Miss Smith who was one of those arrested is the niece of the Lord Mayor of Glasgow.

Mrs Pankhurst & Miss Adela Pankhurst started off on a fortnight's tour in the highlands in the motor. Edinbu[rgh] is a beautiful city. There is Holyrood Palace where Mary Queen of Scots lived & Edinburgh Castle etc - It's very cool up [illegible] is on the sea shore. I had a letter [illegible] ice saying that they were in London.

With Love

Alice

EPHONE No. "503, DUNDEE."

LAMB'S HOTEL, LIMITED.

Dundee Sept 25 1909

Dear Mamma -

I was again arrested Sept 13th. Five of

and were let out in four days as a result. 10,000 people - according to the paper - surrounded Dundee prison the night before we were let out & threatened a fearful riot. We were taken to Lamb's Hotel & were there two days. A doctor & a trained nurse were with us (they are Suffragettes & give their services free of charge) Then a lady who

HOW WOMEN WON THE VOTE

ALICE PAUL, LUCY BURNS, AND THEIR BIG IDEA

Susan Campbell Bartoletti • illustrated by Ziyue Chen

HARPER
An Imprint of HarperCollinsPublishers

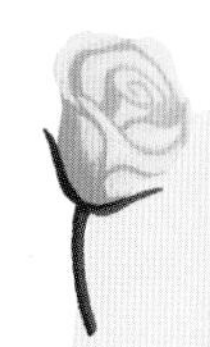

For Erin, my longest, oldest, strongest, amazing-est friend.

—S.C.B.

To my dearest hubby and family, thank you for all the love and support.
And to my darling daughter, may you grow up to be a resilient lady
standing firm in your belief.

—Z.C.

How Women Won the Vote: Alice Paul, Lucy Burns, and Their Big Idea

www.harpercollinschildrens.com

Library of Congress Cataloging-in-Publication Data

Names: Bartoletti, Susan Campbell, author. | Chen, Ziyue, illustrator.
Title: How women won the vote : Alice Paul, Lucy Burns, and their big idea / Susan Campbell Bartoletti ; illustrated by Ziyue Chen.
Description: First edition. | New York : HarperCollins, 2020. | Audience: Ages 8–12 | Audience: Grades 7–9 | Summary: "A history of the iconic first women's march in 1913 and the suffragists who led the way to passing the 19th amendment"— Provided by publisher.
Identifiers: LCCN 2019027293 | ISBN 978-0-06-284130-8 (hardcover)
Subjects: LCSH: Women—Suffrage—United States—History—Juvenile literature. | Suffragists—United States—Juvenile literature. | Feminism—United States—History—Juvenile literature.
Classification: LCC JK1898 .B37 2020 | DDC 324.6/23097309041—dc23
LC record available at https://lccn.loc.gov/2019027293

The artist used pencil, Procreate, and Adobe Photoshop to create the digital illustrations for this book.
Typography by Chelsea Donaldson and Honee Jang
20 21 22 23 24 SCP 10 9 8 7 6 5 4 3 2 1

First Edition

Contents

Part One
Under Arrest!
4

Part Two
A Big Idea
20

Part Three
Parade!
32

Part Four
Boycott!
52

Part Five
Victory!
68

Afterword: More Work to Be Done 72
Before Alice Met Lucy: A Timeline 74
Sources & Notes 76
Further Reading and Image Credits 78
Acknowledgments 79
Index 80

PART ONE

UNDER ARREST!

Cannon Row Police Station
London, England
June 29, 1909

Women milled about the London police station.

It was a warm June night, but the women wore heavy coats as if it were a blustery and cold winter day. Their coats were torn and tattered and covered with dirt, their buttons popped and hanging by a thread, their knees scraped and bloody. Their throats were bruised.

The women—one hundred and eight in all—were under arrest.

WE WANT TO VOTE, TOO.

The trouble started earlier that evening.

Two hundred women had lined up at Caxton Hall to march in a protest parade.

The women were suffragettes. They were protesting because women did not have suffrage, or the right to vote, in Great Britain. And that posed a big problem. They wanted a say in their government.

The suffragettes were marching to Parliament.

Once there, the women would demand to speak to the prime minister.

The suffragettes would demand that members of Parliament—MPs—grant British women the right to vote.

The marchers knew trouble was brewing.
The women had warned one another.

Wear your heaviest, thickest coat.

Wear extra layers. Stuff your clothing with rags.

Wrap yourself with fat spinners yarn and cardboard to protect your body.

Two American women stood with the marchers.
Alice Paul and Lucy Burns did not know each other yet.

Soon Alice and Lucy would meet. Very soon.

At the signal, the all-female band started up.

Drummers rumbled the air.

Fifers shrilled their fifes.

A protest song called "*La Marseillaise*" floated over the marchers.

The drums and the fifes quickened each marcher's heart—and her feet.

Line marshals shouted the orders:

Eyes forward!

Shoulders back!

Move forward!

R WOMEN!

STANDOFF

Along Victoria Street, fifty thousand spectators cheered.

Votes for women! Votes for women!

Other spectators jeered.

Shame! Shame! Go home where you belong!

Hecklers pelted the suffragettes with stones and eggs and rotten fruit and vegetables.

Hecklers didn't believe women should protest. They didn't think women needed the right to vote.

Hecklers said voting should be left up to men.

The suffragettes marched on, eyes forward, shoulders back.

Soon Big Ben and the spires of St. Stephens rose in the distance—

and then a wall of blue.

A fifty-year-old British woman named Emmeline Pankhurst led the suffragettes.

Mrs. Pankhurst had transformed suffragists—women who *asked* for the right to vote—into suffragettes who *demanded* the right to vote.

Head high, chin up, Mrs. Pankhurst and seven suffragettes stepped up to the gate.

"We have come here in the assertion of a right," said Mrs. Pankhurst to the chief inspector of the police.

"The prime minister . . . regrets that he is unable to receive the proposed delegation," said the chief inspector.

Mrs. Pankhurst wouldn't budge. Prime Minister Herbert Henry Asquith often met with men. It was only fair that he meet with women.

The chief inspector didn't budge either.

It was a standoff. And then—

Police officers escort Emmeline Pankhurst to the police station in this undated photograph.

A police officer shoved Mrs. Pankhurst away from the gate.
Mrs. Pankhurst slapped the officer across the face. Twice!
Right away, the chief inspector arrested Mrs. Pankhurst and the seven women.
Mrs. Pankhurst knew what would happen next. Her motto was "Deeds, Not Words."
Every marcher knew the motto.
Even Alice. Even Lucy.

The first row of marchers charged the gate.

The police grabbed the women and hurled them onto the cobblestone street.

The crowd shouted, *Shame! Shame!*

Sixteen times, the women pressed forward.

The police punched and kicked and clubbed the women.

The women curled into balls to shield themselves.

The police arrested one hundred and eight women.

Even the Americans Alice Paul and Lucy Burns.

ALICE MEETS LUCY

At the Cannon Row Police Station, Alice Paul spotted a tall woman who wore a United States pin on her coat.

Another American!

Twenty-four-year-old Alice introduced herself. She was from Mount Laurel, New Jersey.

The woman was twenty-nine-year-old Lucy Burns from Brooklyn, New York.

Alice and Lucy had both sailed across the Atlantic Ocean to study in another country.

While in London, Alice and Lucy met other women like themselves—strong-minded, brave, educated, and rebellious—and got swept up in the Votes for Women movement.

At one o'clock in the morning, the police released the suffragettes.

Later, the charges would be dropped. Alice and Lucy didn't go to jail—this time.

Alice wrote a letter to her mother, who lived in New Jersey. She described the clash with the police: "Dear Mamma—On Tuesday, I went to a deputation to the House of Commons and 108 of us were arrested . . . The scene was one awful nightmare . . . It was a wonder no one was killed. . . ."

Alice's mother wanted her to come home right away.

But Alice wasn't ready to go home. Neither was Lucy.

They were learning how to organize women and how to lead.

Emmeline Pankhurst had invited Alice and Lucy to join protests throughout England and Scotland.

That summer, Alice and Lucy hopped in Mrs. Pankhurst's brand-new motorcar.

In this August 1909 photo, Emmeline Pankhurst sits next to her driver, Vera "Jack" Holme as they leave London for Scotland. The motorcar sported a green body, purple pinstripe, white spokes, and purple and green leather upholstery—all British suffragette colors.

"WE HAD THRILLING TIMES HERE LAST NIGHT," ALICE WROTE HER MOTHER.

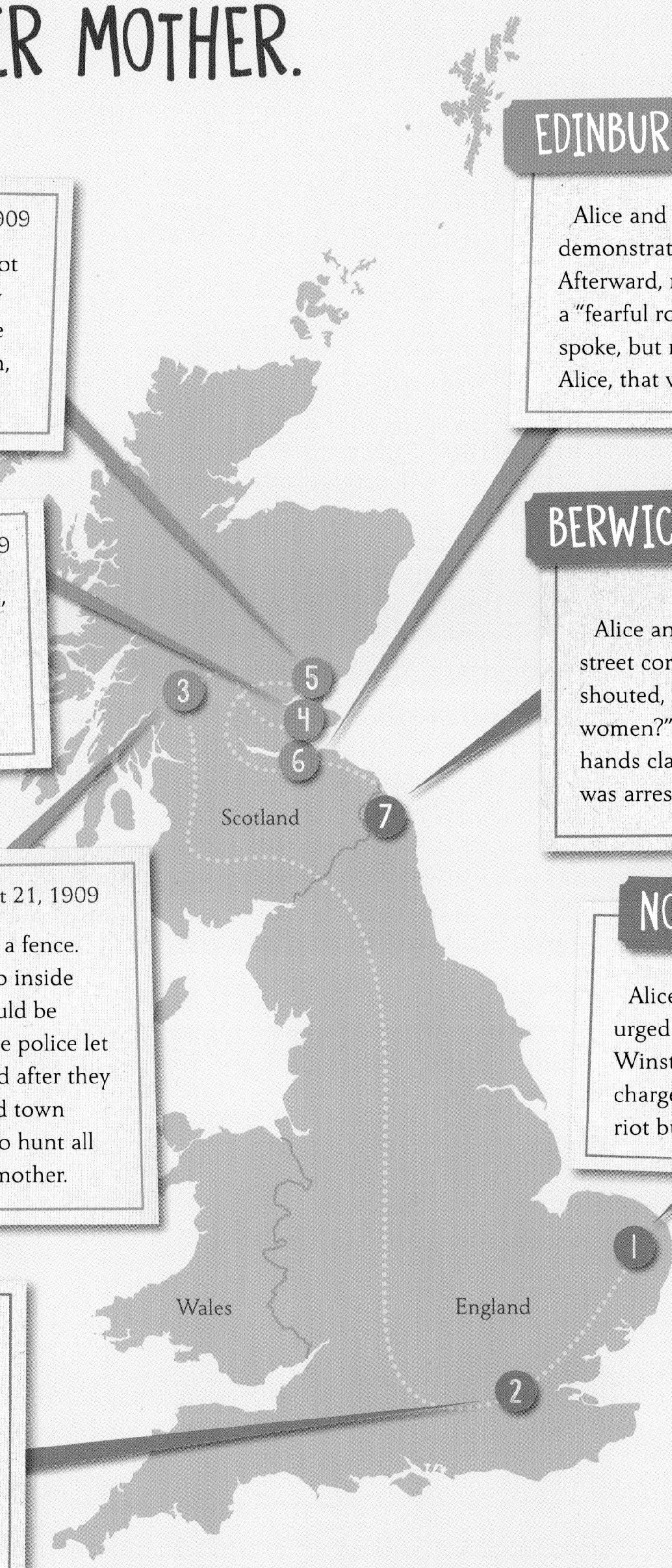

DUNDEE

September 13, 1909

After another arrest, Lucy whipped an inkpot through a police station window; Alice threw stones. Sentenced to ten days in prison, Alice and Lucy staged another hunger strike. Again, the government released them early.

EDINBURGH

October 9, 1909

Alice and Lucy participated in a large demonstration along Princes Street. Afterward, male college students made a "fearful row" as Emmeline Pankhurst spoke, but no students were arrested. To Alice, that wasn't fair.

BURNTISLAND

September 7, 1909

Alice watched boys throw eggs, cabbages, and other rotten fruit and vegetables at a suffrage speaker. "[They] kept it up the whole time," wrote Alice to her mother. No boys were arrested.

BERWICK-UPON-TWEED

October 15, 1909

Alice and Lucy gave speeches on street corners. As an MP spoke, Alice shouted, "What about votes for women?" Police marched her out, hands clasped behind her back. Alice was arrested, but not charged.

GLASGOW

August 21, 1909

Late one night, Lucy boosted Alice over a fence. Alice climbed onto a roof, planning to slip inside St. Andrews Halls, where Lord Crewe would be speaking. A workman caught Alice, but the police let her go. Later, Alice and Lucy were arrested after they rushed the hall entrance. The pair skipped town before court. "It would be a big expense to hunt all over Scotland for us," Alice wrote to her mother.

NORWICH

July 27, 1909

Alice and three other suffragettes urged townspeople to disrupt Winston Churchill's speech. Police charged the women with inciting a riot but didn't jail them.

WEST LONDON

July 30, 1909

After disrupting the Chancellor of the Exchequer's speech, Alice, Lucy, and eleven others were arrested and jailed. The women smashed prison windows and then called a hunger strike. The British government released the starving women early.

News of Alice's arrests reached the United States. A reporter rushed to Alice's mother's house. "I cannot understand how all this came about," Alice's mother told the reporter. "Alice is such a mild-mannered girl."

By November, Alice and Lucy were back in London. One night, Prime Minister Asquith was scheduled to speak at a banquet at the Guildhall.

That evening, Lucy dressed in an elegant gown. She blended in with the banquet guests—until she waved a tiny flag in Winston Churchill's face and scolded him. "How can you dine here while women [suffragettes] are starving in prison?" she said.

The police tossed Lucy out. No one spotted Alice and another suffragette, Amelia Brown, hiding in the balcony.

Asquith began his speech. Amelia stood up and smashed a windowpane with her shoe. Alice shouted, "Votes for Women! Votes for Women!"

The police stormed the balcony. The officers nabbed Alice and Amelia and hauled them before the magistrate.

The magistrate sentenced Alice and Amelia to thirty days in Holloway, a gloomy fortress-like prison for women.

HUNGER STRIKE

At Holloway, guards dragged Alice off to solitary confinement.

Once again, Alice declared a hunger strike.

For four days, Alice refused food.

On the fifth day, prison matrons wrenched Alice out of bed and tied her to a chair.

A prison doctor stuck a long rubber hose as thick as a finger up her nose. He snaked the tube down her throat and into her stomach. He fastened a funnel to the top of the hose. Into the funnel, the doctor poured milk and two raw eggs.

This is called force-feeding.

And it hurt.

Each time Alice refused to eat, she was force-fed again, twice a day.

This time, the British government did not release Alice early.

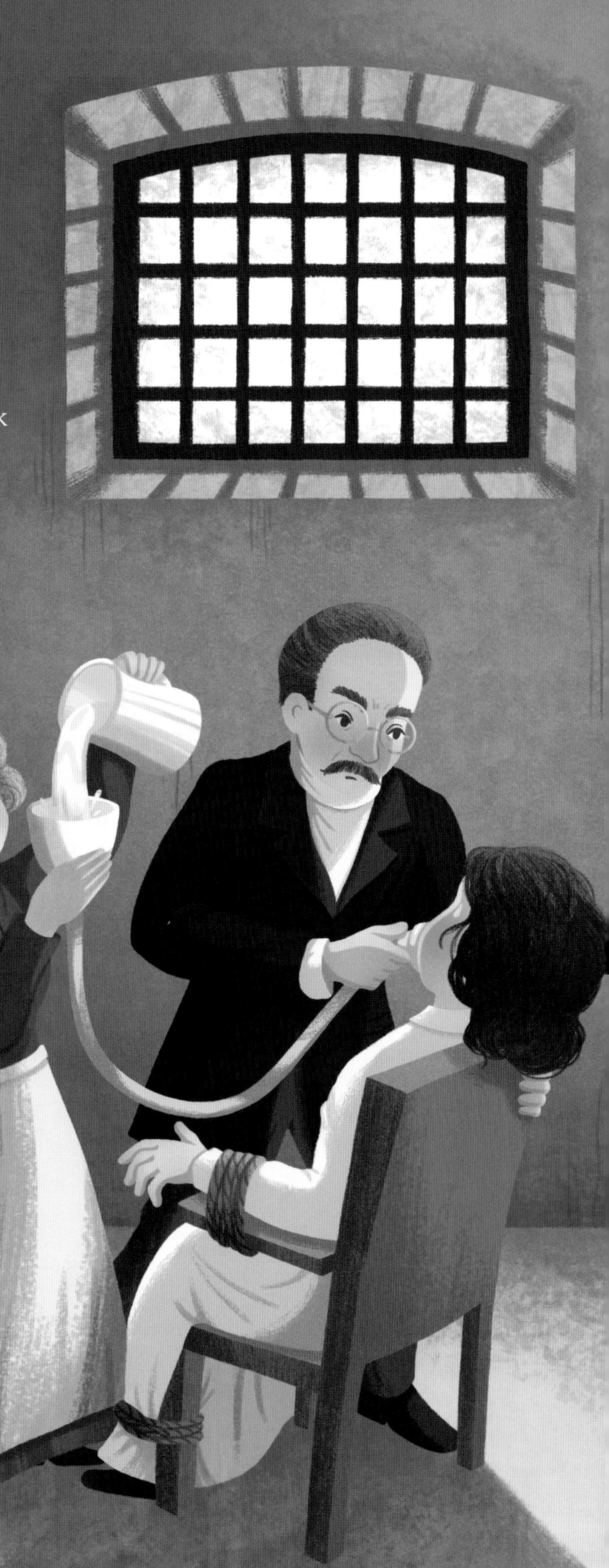

Through broken windowpanes, suffragettes wave to supporters from their cells at Holloway Prison in London.

Thirty days later, Alice was released from prison. It took her one month in bed to recover from the forced feeding.

It was time to go home. Alice booked passage on a steamship to Philadelphia, Pennsylvania.

"I hope I will never have to see my name in the paper again," Alice wrote to her mother.

WON'T TRY TO START SUFFRAGE WAR HERE

Miss Alice Paul, Released from English Prison, Will Sail for Home This Week.

THINKS WOMEN WILL WIN

American Girl Who Served Three Prison Terms for the Cause Holds Faith in the Militant Campaign.

Special Cable to THE NEW YORK TIMES.

LONDON, Jan. 1.—Miss Alice Paul of Philadelphia, the suffragette who on Dec. 9 was released from Holloway Jail after serving one month's imprisonment for her share in the suffragette demonstration at the Lord Mayor's banquet at the Guildhall, will sail for

New York Times, January 2, 1910.

PART TWO

A BIG IDEA

Philadelphia, Pennsylvania
1910–1912

It took fifteen days for the SS Haverford to cross the stormy Atlantic Ocean.
Somewhere over the Atlantic, on January 11, Alice turned twenty-five.
At dusk, nine days later, the steamship arrived in Philadelphia.
A thinner-than-ever but smiling Alice waited until last to walk down the gangplank.
Her mother and youngest brother, Parry, stood at the bottom.
So did reporters.

PURPLE STOOD FOR DIGNITY

Home for good, Alice splurged on a purple velvet hat. Purple stood for dignity—the dignity that the right to vote would give women.

Alice joined the National American Woman Suffrage Association, or NAWSA. She wore the hat to suffrage luncheons and meetings.

A popular speaker, Alice defended the British suffragettes and their protests and hunger strikes. "You must resort to unusual tactics," said Alice, "to wake them up over there."

The next summer, 1911, Alice organized women in Philadelphia. She planned outdoor suffrage meetings throughout the city.

Alice needed a fiery speaker for the events.

Someone witty and sharp and brave.

Someone who could rally working women to the suffrage cause.

Alice needed Lucy.

New York Times,
December 10, 1909.

MISS PAUL DESCRIBES FEEDING BY FORCE

American Suffragette in Holloway Jail Lay Abed During Whole of 30-Day Sentence.

REFUSED PRISON CLOTHES

Three Wardresses and Two Doctors Held Her While Food Was Injected Through Nostrils—Now Released.

YORK TIMES.

A friend attributed Alice Paul's persuasive powers to her "great earnest childlike eyes."

That July, Lucy was home from London, visiting her family. She agreed to help Alice for one week.

At the first meeting, Lucy fired up the crowd. Men could vote. Why not women? Soon three hundred people gathered around.

A policeman rounded the corner. Lucy spotted him. So did Alice and her small band of suffragists.

Alice had broken the law. She had failed to get a permit from city hall to hold a street meeting.

Lucy kept talking. Alice grew excited. An arrest would make the newspapers. The publicity would drum up sympathy for the women and draw bigger crowds.

The policeman did not arrest Alice or Lucy or any other suffragist.

That week, Lucy gave four more speeches. She returned to Brooklyn, and then sailed back to London.

Alice wanted more. More rallies. Bigger crowds.

She needed to draw more women to the meetings.

But horses and carts and drivers and signs cost money. The suffrage treasury had a tight budget.

Alice had an idea. Something suffragettes had done in London.

Chalk.

The chalk worked. Each night the crowds grew larger and larger.

By the end of the summer, two thousand people filled Independence Square, eager to hear suffrage speakers at the rally. It was time to think bigger than Philadelphia.

The next year, 1912, Lucy returned home for good. Alice and Lucy visited one another. They talked about suffrage. For sixty-four years, American women had begged their states to let them vote. What did that begging get them?

Nine out of forty-eight states: Wyoming, Colorado, Utah, Idaho, Washington, California, Arizona, Kansas, Oregon—and one territory, Montana. That was all.

Alice had an idea. A big idea.

HELLO, PRESIDENT WILSON

In November a Democrat named Woodrow Wilson was elected president.

Good riddance, President William Howard Taft, who called women too "hysterical" to vote.

Hello, President Wilson, who called liberty "a fundamental necessity for the life of the soul."

Surely Woodrow Wilson would favor liberty for women.

WILLIAM HOWARD TAFT

WOODROW WILSON

Alice told Lucy her big idea:

It's time to take our fight to Washington.

It's time to demand a federal amendment to the Constitution.

It's time to guarantee and protect a woman's right to vote, once and for all.

It's time for a—

In the United States Capitol, shown here, members of the Senate and House of Representatives discuss, debate, and vote on new laws and amendments.

Parade!

A parade of women!

Thousands of women—marching, marching, marching down Pennsylvania Avenue.

With flags. And floats. And bands. And banners. And brigades.

And a giant sign that demands votes for women.

This parade would be the biggest, best, most glorious suffrage parade of all.

It was time to show the country that women could not—and would not—be ignored.

Alice predicted one year until victory.

Lucy could bank on that.

And Lucy did.

THINGS A SUFFRAGE PARADE NEEDS

MONEY

A parade costs money. The Treasury will not contribute one dollar, said Anna Howard Shaw, the president of NAWSA. Don't send us any bills.

Alice said, We'll raise every dollar ourselves.

ANNA HOWARD SHAW

ELEGANCE & SHINE

NAWSA leaders wanted a parade with elegance and shine, not clashes like the marches in England and Scotland. American women were suffragists, not suffragettes.

Alice agreed. So did Lucy.

A COMMITTEE & VOLUNTEERS

NAWSA leaders appointed Alice parade chairman and Lucy as vice-chairman. Alice and Lucy recruited remarkable women.

A PLACE TO LIVE

In early December 1912, Alice arrived in Washington. She moved into a small room on the third floor of a boardinghouse for women.

HEADQUARTERS

Alice rented a small basement office at 1420 F Street—a short walk from the White House.

PUBLICITY

Volunteers pounded away on typewriters, writing news articles and letters and invitations for women to march. The women held street meetings and luncheons and teas to promote the parade.

PARADE ROUTE

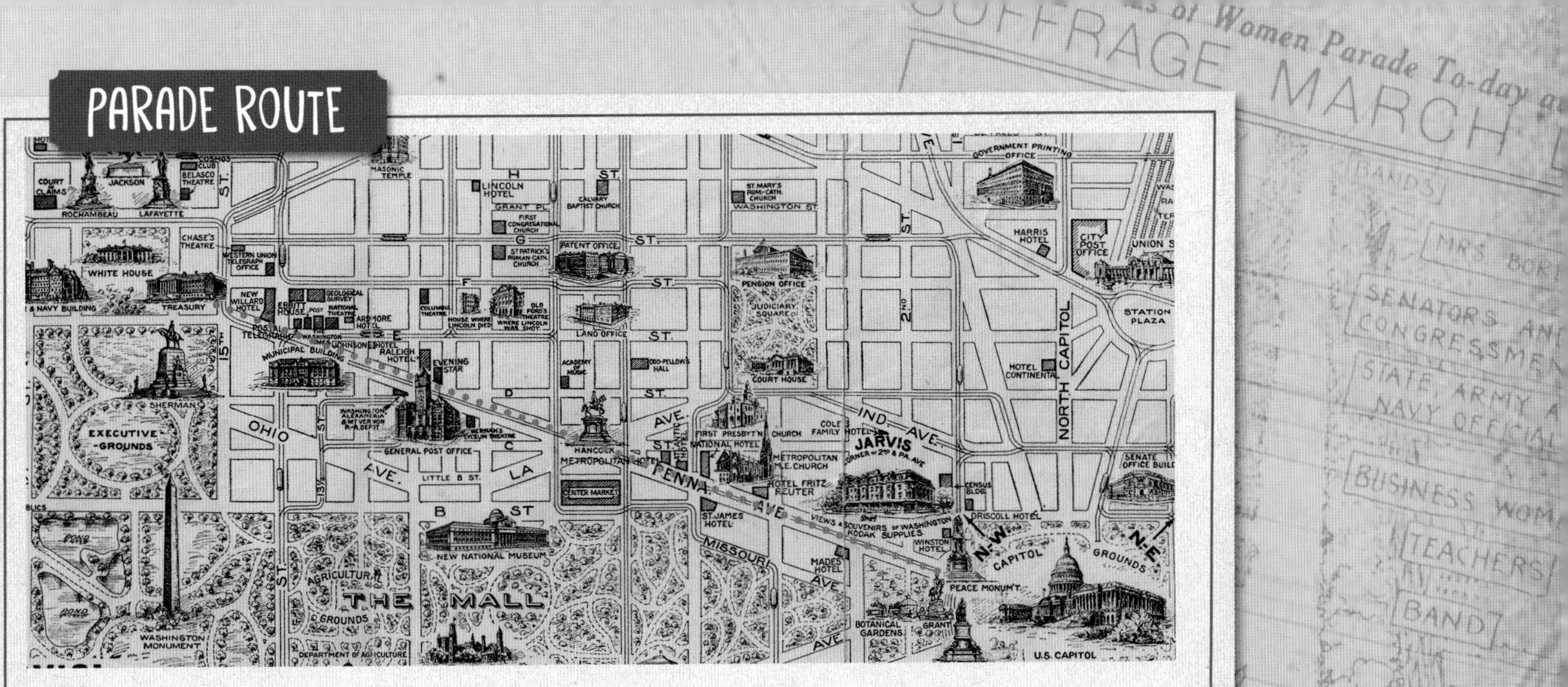

On March 3, 1913—the day before Woodrow Wilson's inauguration—the massive parade would flow up Pennsylvania Avenue, from the Capitol to the Treasury Building. An estimated 150,000 people would pour into Washington for the inauguration festivities.

A PAGEANT DESIGNER

Hazel MacKaye, a professional theater dramatist, agreed to stage a pageant that celebrated the ideals of American democracy at the Treasury Building. She called the pageant "The Allegory."

HAZEL MACKAYE

A GIANT SIGN

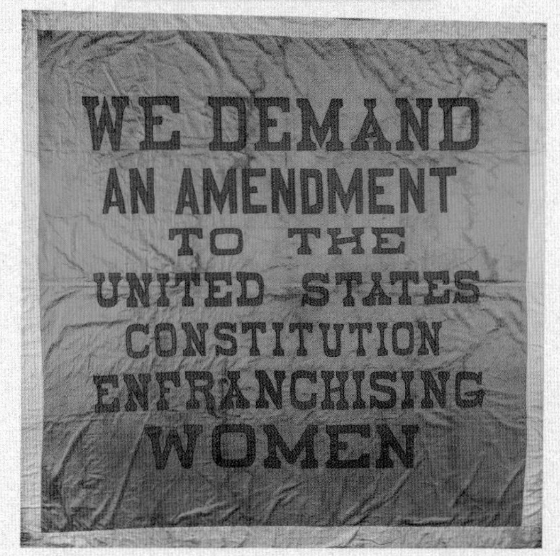

The parade would begin with the women's demand for a federal suffrage amendment.

A HERALD ON A HORSE

The popular lawyer Inez Milholland fought for the rights of workers, women, children, and the poor. As the lead herald, Inez would deliver the suffragists' demand to the president and Congress.

INEZ MILHOLLAND

PARADE PERMIT

This time, Alice wasn't risking arrest. She planned a peaceful, beautiful, and newsworthy parade—one that would make the front pages of newspapers around the country.

A RIGHT TO THE AVENUE

Richard H. Sylvester, shown here, was appointed superintendent of the Washington police in 1898.

At police headquarters, Alice met with Richard H. Sylvester, the superintendent of police. The fifty-three-year-old superintendent couldn't believe his ears. This woman wanted a permit for a parade of women! On Pennsylvania Avenue! On Monday, March 3, the day before Woodrow Wilson's inauguration!

No other day would do, Alice said.

You're asking for trouble, Sylvester warned Alice. That day, out-of-town "riff-raff" and "roughscuff" would fill the seedy saloons along Pennsylvania Avenue.

Sylvester told Alice that he could only spare one hundred police officers.

Alice wanted more police, but Sylvester said no. No extra police. No parade. No Pennsylvania Avenue. No March 3. He would not allow it.

Alice left Sylvester's office empty-handed.

Back at headquarters, Alice telephoned the wives of senators and congressmen. She dashed out letters to prominent women and business leaders. She sent editorials to newspapers and called reporters.

We have a "right to the Avenue," Alice told them. Men have marched on the avenue. Why not women?

Day after day, Sylvester's telephone rang. Important men and women knocked on his office door. Letters poured into his office. Newspapers printed editorials and articles.

LET THE WOMEN HAVE THE AVENUE FOR THEIR PARADE!

Sylvester caved. He granted Alice the parade permit.

At headquarters, suffragists cheered. The women unfurled purple-white-and-green banners. For Alice, it was a double celebration. Lucy had arrived in Washington.

Lucy Burns (second from left)

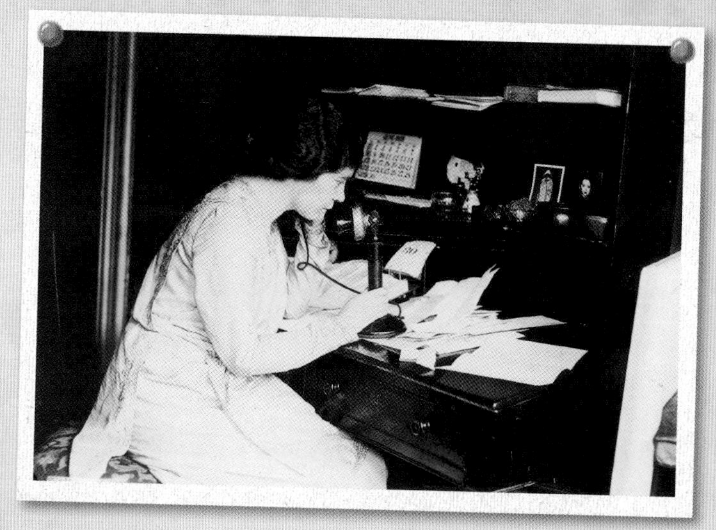

Alice Paul

VOTES FOR WOMEN

Nellie Bly

Helen Keller

Margaret Vale

PART THREE
PARADE!

Washington, DC
January–March 1913

Lucy got busy, organizing meetings and giving speeches on street corners.

Alice made telephone calls and responded to letters from women who wanted to march.

The list of marchers grew longer. Famous women such as the journalist Nellie Bly; activist Helen Keller; classical dancer Florence Fleming Noyes; actress Margaret Vale—who was also Woodrow Wilson's niece—and a Piegan Blackfoot woman named Dawn Mist all wanted to march or ride a float or perform in the pageant.

There would even be a men's section, led by Richmond P. Hobson, a hero from the Spanish-American War.

Florence Fleming Noyes

Dawn Mist

Richmond P. Hobson

"I SHALL NOT MARCH AT ALL . . ."

Nellie May Quander

Mary Church Terrell

In mid-January, a schoolteacher named Nellie May Quander wanted to know if black women might march. Nellie was president of Alpha Kappa Alpha, a sorority of black women at Howard University.

So did the newly formed Delta Sigma Theta sorority at Howard University.

So did Civil Rights leaders Ida B. Wells-Barnett and Mary Church Terrell and Carrie Williams Clifford. They encouraged other black women to apply.

But when black women showed up at suffrage offices to register for the parade, white women told them that the registry clerk was not available.

Such racial discrimination was not new. Many NAWSA members had long discriminated against black women to win the support of southern white women and white men.

Alice offered a compromise: black women could march together at the back of the parade.

Ida B. Wells

Absolutely not. "We do not wish to enter if we must meet with discrimination," wrote Nellie May Quander.

Ida B. Wells-Barnett wanted to march with women from her home state. "I shall not march at all," she said, "unless I can march under the Illinois banner."

Telegrams and letters poured into Alice's office. Some came from white women who threatened not to march with black women; others accused Alice of discrimination.

Finally NAWSA's national secretary wrote to Alice, telling her: "The suffrage movement stands for enfranchising every single woman in the United States." Four days before the parade, NAWSA leaders sent Alice a telegram. *Let black women march.*

Alice didn't want negative publicity. Ever so quietly, she accepted applications from black suffragists.

Activist Nannie Helen Burroughs, shown here holding a Woman's National Baptist Convention banner, encouraged black women's church groups and clubs to march.

TROUBLE

These Boy Scouts were among the fifteen hundred scouts who traveled to Washington to help during the inauguration festivities.

It was now two days before the parade. Thousands of suffragists were pouring into Washington from across the country—by train, trolley, bus, automobile, and horse-drawn carriage, and on foot.

Inauguration-goers arrived in droves, too. The visitors had booked every hotel, boarding house, and lodging house. They filled private houses in the city and outskirts.

Alice and Lucy counted on the visitors to turn out for the suffrage parade.

After all, who wouldn't love a suffrage parade?

Anti-suffragists, that's who.

Led by "General" Rosalie Jones, sixteen women hiked two hundred and sixty miles from New York to Washington, DC.

On Pennsylvania Avenue, crowds watch the hikers' celebrated arrival. The hikers can be seen waving American flags and marching behind the suffragists on white horses.

Vote NO
n Woman Suffrage

:CAUSE 90% of the women either do not want it, or *do not care.*

ECAUSE it means *competition* of women with men instead of *co-operation.*

ECAUSE 80% of the women eligible to vote are married and can only double or annul their husbands' votes.

BECAUSE it can be of no benefit commensurate with the additional expense involved.

BECAUSE in some States more voting women than voting men will place the Government under petticoat rule.

BECAUSE it is unwise to risk the good we already have for the evil which may occur.

A woman watches men reading anti-suffrage literature.

Powerful, wealthy women and men led the anti-suffrage movement. They claimed woman suffrage would hurt the home, the family, and the country.

Anti-suffragists opened their own headquarters. When they filled their windows with nasty cartoons that mocked the suffragists, they found them smeared with mud. Right away, they accused the suffragists.

Bitter letters flew between the two offices until Alice stepped in. "This is a woman's movement," Alice scolded her volunteers, "and we will not attack any woman with words."

More trouble loomed. Anna Howard Shaw refused to march under the suffragette purple-white-and-green banner. To appease her, Alice ordered purple-white-and-yellow banners. Georgetown University students plotted to release six thousand white mice along the parade route.

Mice didn't frighten Alice. Inadequate police protection did.

Twice, Alice asked Sylvester for more police officers.

Twice, Sylvester refused.

Instead, he asked a Boy Scout commissioner to send scouts.

VOTE
NO
ON WOMAN SUFFRAGE

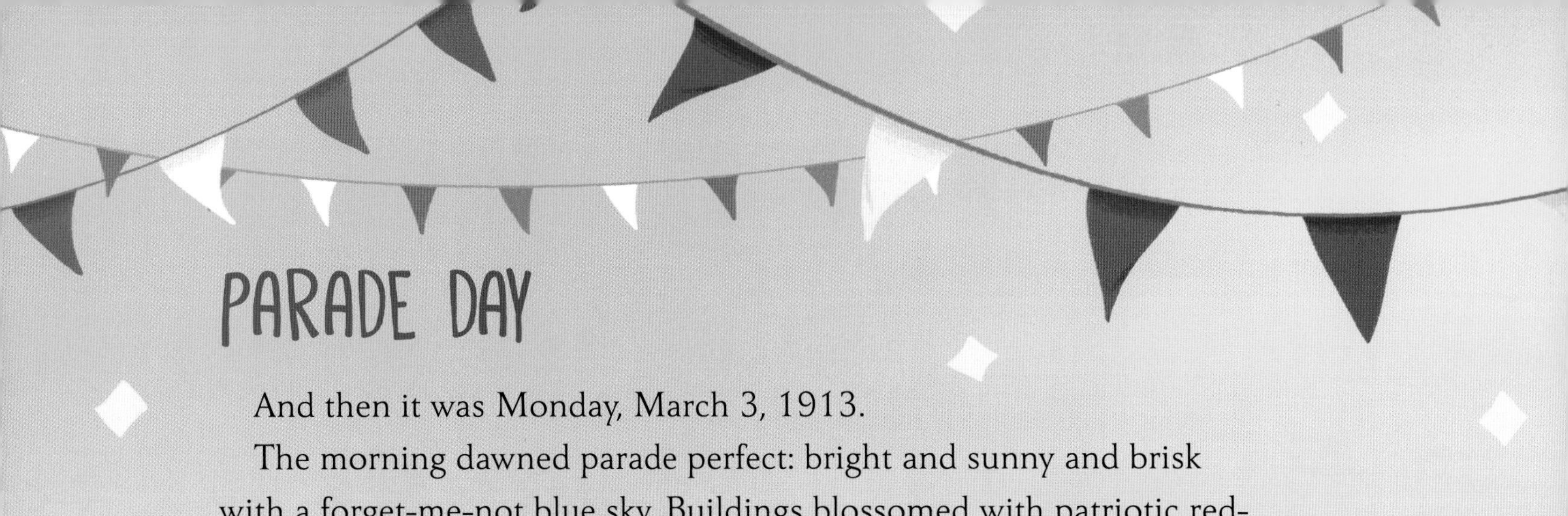

PARADE DAY

And then it was Monday, March 3, 1913.

The morning dawned parade perfect: bright and sunny and brisk with a forget-me-not blue sky. Buildings blossomed with patriotic red-white-and-blue bunting for the next day's inauguration festivities.

Alice and Lucy headed to the staging area near the Capitol, passing boisterous spectators already lining the avenue.

The Capitol grounds and side streets bloomed, too, with flags and pennants and banners and women in colorful costumes.

Band members warmed up, filling the air with drumrolls and pipes and tweets and blares.

Men shouted as they positioned horse-drawn floats and chariots.

Wagon wheels creaked. Horses snorted and whinnied and stamped their feet.

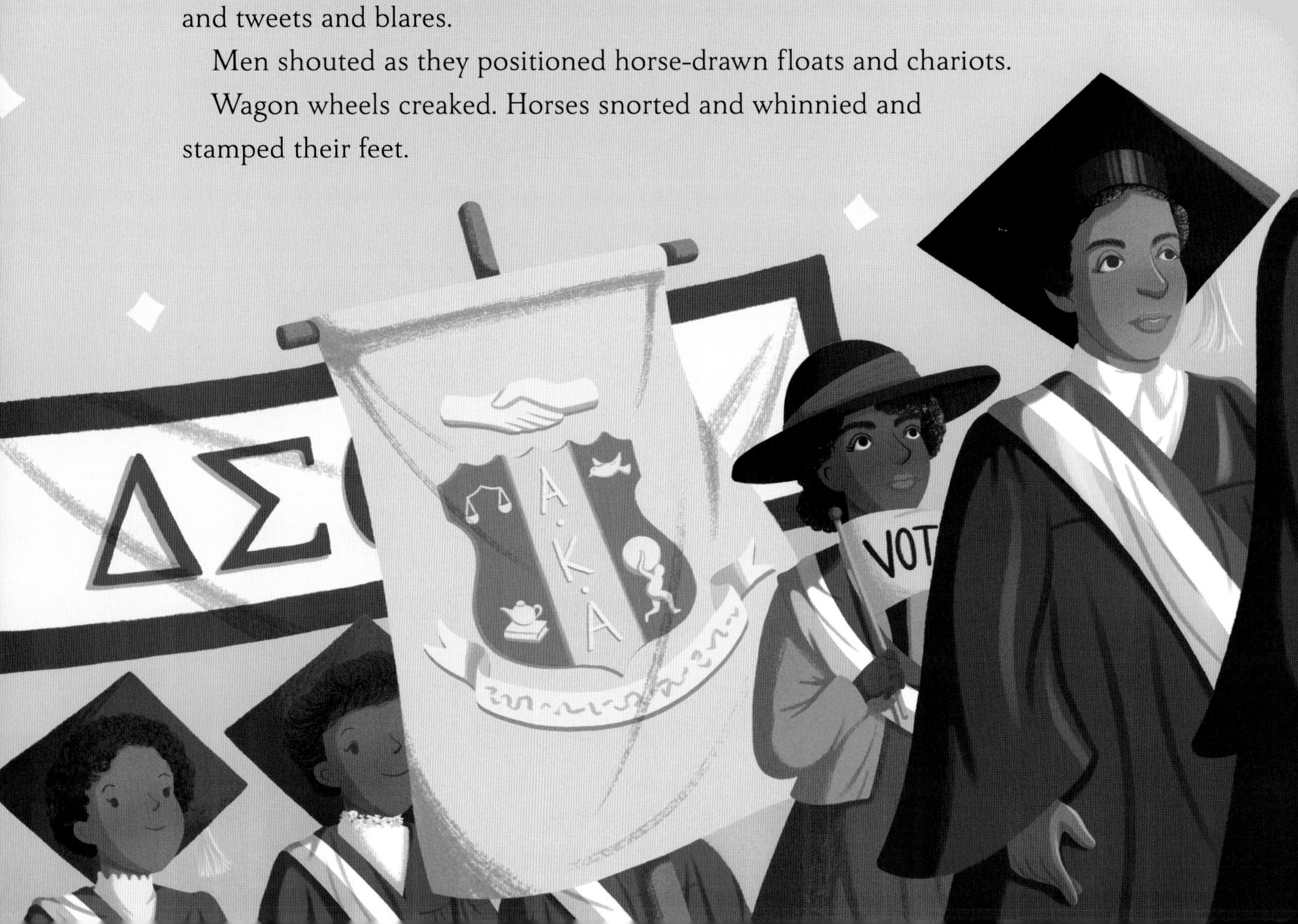

Today Alice didn't wear her purple hat. She wore her university cap and gown. She and Lucy took their places with the college women. So did Nellie May Quander and Mary Church Terrell and women from the Alpha and Delta sororities. Carrie Williams Clifford stood with a unit of black professional women.

Wearing brown cloaks and boots, "General" Rosalie Jones and her sixteen hikers mustered behind a band. Ida B. Wells-Barnett joined the Illinois delegation, but several white women ordered her to leave. "If the Illinois women do not take a stand now in this great democratic parade, then the colored women are lost," said Ida.

But the Illinois women would not take a stand.

Insulted, Ida left.

By three o'clock, two hundred and fifty thousand eager spectators jammed Pennsylvania Avenue. They crammed every window, every rooftop, every inch of sidewalk.

And then it was time. Inez Milholland rode her white charger to the Peace Monument in front of the Capitol.

Behind Inez, the first float—the Great Demand—rolled into place with a message to President Wilson and Congress: "We Demand an Amendment to the United States Constitution Enfranchising the Women of the Country."

Twenty-five minutes later, a shot rang out, signaling the parade to begin.

EYES FORWARD!

SHOULDERS BACK!

MOVE FORWARD!

PROCESSION

Over five thousand suffragists, nine bands, four mounted brigades, and twenty-six floats made their way down Pennsylvania Avenue.

THE LEAD HERALD

Dressed as a warrior, Inez Milholland symbolized the femininity, intelligence, and strength of the suffrage cause.

THE HOMEMAKERS

From all over the country, from all professions and all walks of life, women came together in a show of pride, solidarity, and power. Here, members of the Homemakers Association march.

VOTES FOR WOMEN

FUTURE VOTERS

Young suffragists passed the NAWSA stand.

A CRUSADER

Mid-march, Ida B. Wells-Barnett stepped out from the crowded sidewalk and joined the Illinois delegation. "I am doing it for the future of my whole race," said Ida, as were the fifty other black women who marched.

FLOATS

Horse-drawn floats rolled past spectators. The floats represented women throughout history, including "Women of the Bible Lands."

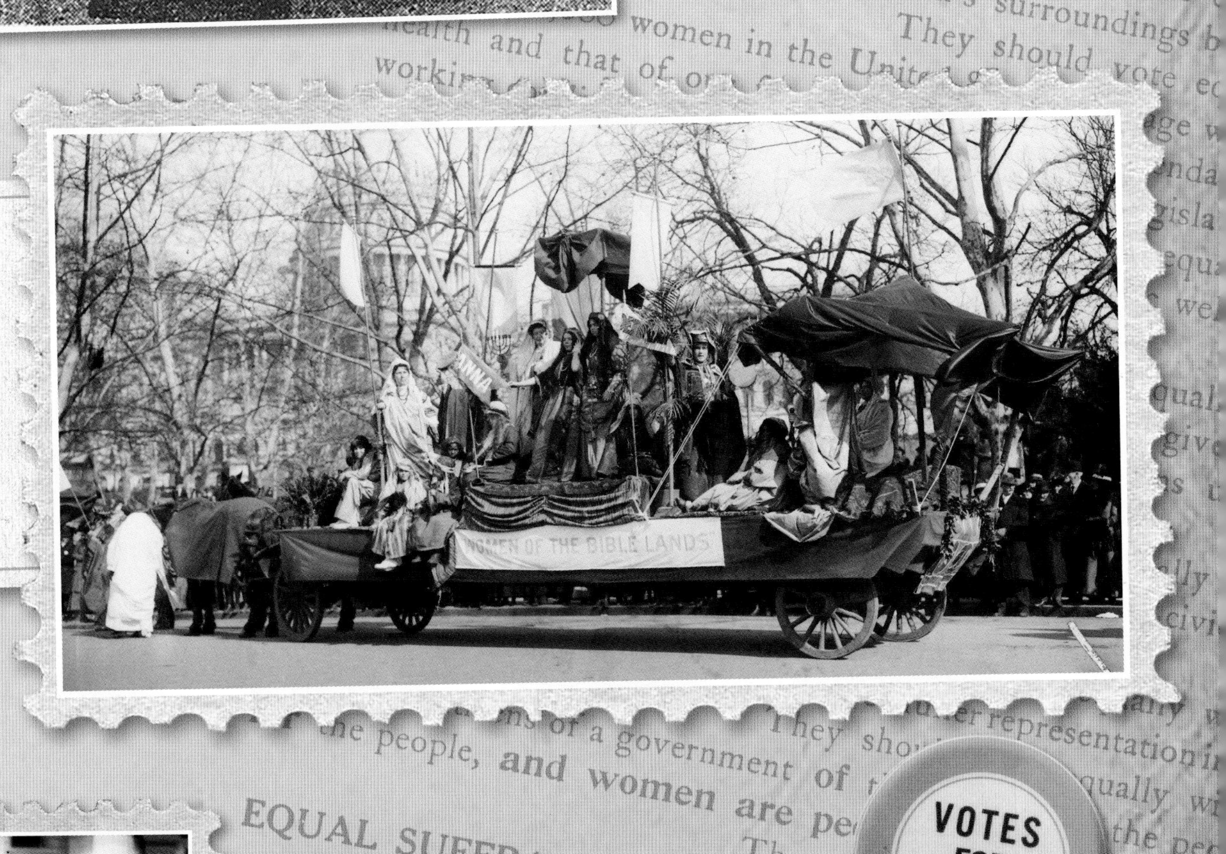

A PAGEANT

VOTES FOR WOMEN

At the other end of Pennsylvania Avenue, one thousand people filled the grandstands outside the Treasury Building. As a band played, the massive doors swung open. A German actress, Hedwig Reicher, struck a pose in the doorway. She was performing the role of Columbia, the goddess of American Liberty.

Columbia walked down the broad marble steps. She signaled the women and girls waiting behind the tall columns.

One at a time, women ran out, each one dressed as an American ideal: Charity, Justice, Plenty, and Liberty. Behind the women, young girls scattered rose petals. At the top of the steps, Peace released a white dove that soared into the bright blue sky. The last virtue, Hope, danced down the steps, followed by girls wearing rainbow-colored dresses. At the bottom, Hope and her attendants suspended golden balls above their heads.

The last ideal, Hope, and her attendants in a dance.

One hundred women and girls froze in place, forming a living tableau, waiting to join the marchers.

Where were they?

A March wind gusted through. The tableau performers shivered in their filmy costumes and sandaled feet.

Something was clearly wrong.

"GIRLS, GET OUT YOUR HAT PINS!"

Farther up Pennsylvania Avenue, the massive crowd had turned ugly.

Men pressed against the rope barriers. Many smelled like the seedy saloons Sylvester had warned Alice about.

The rowdies hooted and hollered. "A disgrace to women!"

"The place of women is in the home!"

"I hope the sidewalk falls through!"

Realizing the danger, a marcher called out, "Girls, get out your hat pins! They are going to rush us."

And rush the men did.

Mobs broke through the ropes and surged into the street.

They tripped the suffragists and shoved and slapped and pinched and spat tobacco juice on the women. Others snatched banners and grabbed the reins of the horses and swarmed over the floats.

Alice and Lucy and other marchers called for the police to help, but the mob was too unruly and the police too few to control the crowd.

Without enough police for crowd control, spectators spill into the street.

STEP BACK!

Alice and Lucy shoved men out of the way. Women riding the floats kicked the men who grabbed their feet. On horseback, women charged into the mobs, trying to open the clogged street.

The Boy Scouts sprang into action. Wielding staves, the scouts forced rioters to the curb.

Some spectators helped. National Guardsmen visiting from Massachusetts pushed back the crowd. Maryland University students laced arms, forming a human barricade.

Police and other drivers guided automobiles into the street to clear a path.

And then the Fort Myer cavalry galloped in.

Determined to finish what they had begun, the women clasped hands, closed ranks, and marched onward to the Treasury Building.

As Inez Milholland rode into view on her white charger, the tableau performers raced to join the parade.

With elegance and shine, the suffragists paraded past cheering spectators in the grandstands.

PART FOUR
BOYCOTT!

Washington, DC
1913–1920

Woodrow Wilson settled into the Oval Office at the White House. Two weeks later, on March 17, Alice Paul and four other suffragists called on the fifty-seven-year-old president.

Wilson had agreed to meet with the women for ten minutes, so Alice got right to the point. As president, would he use his influence to convince his fellow Democrats in Congress to support a federal suffrage amendment?

Wilson would not budge.

Neither would Congress.

"Somebody has to make the home and who is going to do it if the women don't?" Wilson would later tell a friend.

Alice needed a bigger, bolder plan—a boycott.

Four million women had the right to vote in nine states. Alice called on those women to vote against Democrats in congressional elections.

Boycott! Boycott Democrats!

The boycott angered NAWSA leaders such as Anna Howard Shaw and Carrie Chapman Catt.

Call off the boycott, said Catt. *It's unladylike. It could turn supporters against us.*

In July 1913, a motorcade heads to Washington, DC, to deliver petitions for a federal suffrage amendment to US senators at the Capitol.

Mabel Vernon speaks to a
Mabel proved to be a fearless s
organizer, fundraiser, and h

Wearing leather goggles and a s
sash, Lucy flies over Seattle, sho
the city with suffrage le

On steam trains such as this one, suffragists head to western states to encourage enfranchised women to boycott Democrats.

Alice refused. So did Lucy.

Alice and Lucy and other suffragists headed out across the country. Alice's friend Mabel Vernon quit her job teaching to help.

In cities and towns, the women opened new suffrage offices, hoisted pennants, unfurled banners, staged rallies, gave rousing speeches, and collected signatures on petitions.

Good news! Twenty-three Democrats lost in the November 1914 congressional elections. Two more states—Nevada and Montana—granted women the right to vote, bringing the total to eleven.

Alice wanted more.

In 1916, NWP suffragists gather in Chicago to demonstrate against Woodrow Wilson as he delivers a speech.

The friction between Alice and Lucy and NAWSA leaders grew.

Fed up, Alice and Lucy split from NAWSA. The two women founded a new political party, the National Woman's Party (NWP). The NWP had one goal: to win a federal suffrage amendment.

The NWP moved its headquarters to Cameron House on Lafayette Square across the street from the White House. In 1916, when Woodrow Wilson campaigned for reelection, the NWP suffragists fanned out again, increasing their attacks.

Boycott! Boycott President Wilson!

HOW LONG MUST THIS GO ON?

In September 1916, Inez Milholland set out on a suffrage speaking tour. Over thirty days, she would visit nine western states and give fifty speeches.

At each stop, the popular lawyer drew thousands. But Inez wasn't feeling well. Throughout the trip she grew weaker. From Utah, she contacted Alice, who urged her not to cancel. Just sit on the stage. Let someone else speak.

Inez pushed on to Los Angeles, California, where she collapsed and later died. Her sister Vida scribbled her last words: "president wilson how long must this go on no liberty." She cabled them to Alice.

Suffragists packed Inez's memorial service. As the service ended, an organ burst out in the protest song that had united Alice and Lucy six years earlier—"*La Marseillaise*."

SUFFS HECKLE THE PRESIDENT

On December 5, 1916, ten days after Inez died, Mabel Vernon wrapped herself in a bulky winter coat and headed into the Capitol with Lucy Burns and eight other suffragists. Despite the boycott, President Wilson had won reelection, and now he was going to address Congress.

A guard escorted the women to front row seats in the balcony.

No guard or Secret Service agent seemed to recognize Mabel or Lucy. The previous July, Mabel had ambushed Wilson at an outdoor speech. Twice, Mabel shouted, "Why do you oppose the national enfranchisement of women?" before the Secret Service whisked her away.

And now Mabel was about to strike again.

The suffragists listened as Wilson urged Congress to grant voting rights to men who lived in Puerto Rico. The words "Puerto Rico" were Mabel's cue.

Mabel yanked a bundle from her coat—a large yellow silk banner. She and four other women gripped the banner and flung it over the railing.

The startled president looked up at the fluttering cloth.

Senators and representatives turned toward the balcony. The floor buzzed. "Suffragists!" the lawmakers hissed.

"We feel that we did our duty today," said Lucy, "and we never should have forgiven ourselves had we overlooked it."

Over the coming days, the NWP suffragists busied themselves choosing the best words for more banners.

BAD MANNERS AND MAD BANNERS

On January 10, 1917, a dozen women spilled out of Cameron House. Each woman carried a tall banner demanding the federal amendment. Mabel Vernon led the women to the White House gates.

Day after day, six days a week, for two months, women took turns standing as silent as statues through snow, sleet, wind, and rain. Mary Church Terrell and her daughter took a turn, too.

Carrie Chapman Catt called the pickets "childish." Men called the women "silly," "crazy," and "pathological." In a letter to a newspaper, a critic scolded the women, saying they had "bad manners and mad banners."

Alice's mother didn't approve. "Dear Alice," she wrote. "I wish to make a protest against the methods you are adopting in annoying the President. . . . I hope thee will call it off."

Alice would not. On March 4, the night before Wilson's second inauguration, hundreds of women staged a grand picket, circling the White House.

President Wilson ordered guards to lock the White House gates.

NWP suffragists picket the White House. The banner bears Inez Milholland's last words.

Most days President Wilson ignored the pickets.

As he passed through the gates, Wilson stared straight ahead or turned his head. Other days, he smiled and tipped his hat.

But the president couldn't ignore the banners. The banners quoted his book of campaign speeches, *The New Freedom*. The women shamed him with his own words.

Wilson also could not ignore the Great War raging in Europe.

For over two years, the United States had remained neutral. But by April 2, 1917, Germany had sunk or damaged sixteen US merchant ships. Wilson asked Congress to declare war on Germany. It was a war, said Wilson, to make the world "safe for democracy."

Suffragists fumed. How dare the president call for democracy overseas when democracy was denied to women at home!

President Wilson, wearing a top hat, strides through the White House gates.

On June 20, Lucy Burns and fifty-year-old Dora Lewis held a ten-foot banner outside the White House.

It stated: WE, THE WOMEN OF AMERICA, TELL YOU THAT AMERICA IS NOT A DEMOCRACY. TWENTY MILLION AMERICAN WOMEN ARE DENIED THE RIGHT TO VOTE.

A crowd gathered, outraged at the banner's words. "Treason!" shouted several men. "Shame!" Some hurled rotten fruit at the women.

A man named Walter Timms pulled a penknife from his pocket. "Come on, boys, let's tear that thing down," he called.

Lucy and Dora did not fight back as Timms slashed the fabric. Police stood by as other men snapped the poles and tore the cloth.

The next day, Lucy and twenty-five-year-old Katharine Morey carried a second banner, same as the first, to the White House. A crowd shredded that banner, too. Wilson and his administration decided to remove the pickets. The police chief telephoned Alice to warn her.

SHUT UP THERE, YOU!

The next day, on June 22, the police arrested Lucy and Katharine Morey and charged them with obstructing traffic. Over the next three weeks, the police arrested sixty-two women.

At each trial, the police court judge, Alexander R. Mullowney, banged his gavel. *Guilty! Pay a twenty-five-dollar fine or go to jail!* The women chose jail.

Undaunted, the rest of the women continued to picket. As summer turned to fall, the infuriated judge handed down longer and longer sentences. He sent some women to Washington's District Jail. Others he sent to the Occoquan Workhouse in Virginia.

Lucy Burns was sentenced to three days, then sixty days, and then six months in the Occoquan Workhouse. After her second arrest, Alice was sentenced to seven months in the District Jail. Before leaving, Alice wrote to her mother, telling her not to worry, saying, "It will merely be a delightful rest."

Carrying a banner, Alice Paul leaves NWP headquarters and heads to the White House.

Suffragists arrive at the District Jail in Washington, DC.

At the Occoquan Workhouse, the guards expected the women to wear the prison uniforms and work in the sewing room, but they refused. Infuriated, the guards beat and kicked the women and hurled them into cells.

Lucy called out, asking each woman if she was hurt. "Shut up there, you," shouted Raymond Whittaker, the workhouse superintendent. He shackled Lucy's hands to an overhead iron bar.

At the District Jail, officials isolated Alice in the psychiatric ward.

Alice called a hunger strike. The strike spread. Prison doctors force-fed Alice, Lucy, and the other hunger strikers three times a day.

Lawyers fought for the suffragists. On November 23, 1917, the women were released on a technicality. They should have served their time in the District Jail, not the Occoquan Workhouse.

As soon as they could, the suffragists returned to the picket line. The attacks and arrests and prison sentences continued.

Lucy sits in her cell at the Occoquan Workhouse.

A CHANGE OF HEART

The world was changing. In 1918, Britain would grant voting rights to qualified women over the age of thirty. Later that year, Germany would surrender, ending the Great War.

On January 10, 1918, suffrage headquarters buzzed with news. President Wilson had a change of heart. He now wanted his fellow Democrats in Congress to vote in favor of the amendment.

It would be "an act of right and justice to the women of the country and the world."

After several votes, the amendment passed the House of Representatives on May 21, 1919, and the Senate two weeks later.

Now the amendment had to be ratified by the states. Thirty-six out of forty-eight states had to vote yes.

Once again, NWP suffragists pressured President Wilson to rally his party. This time, they targeted Republicans, too.

Each time a state voted "yes," Alice stitched a star on the ratification banner. By summer, 1920, the banner had thirty-five stars. The suffragists needed one more state.

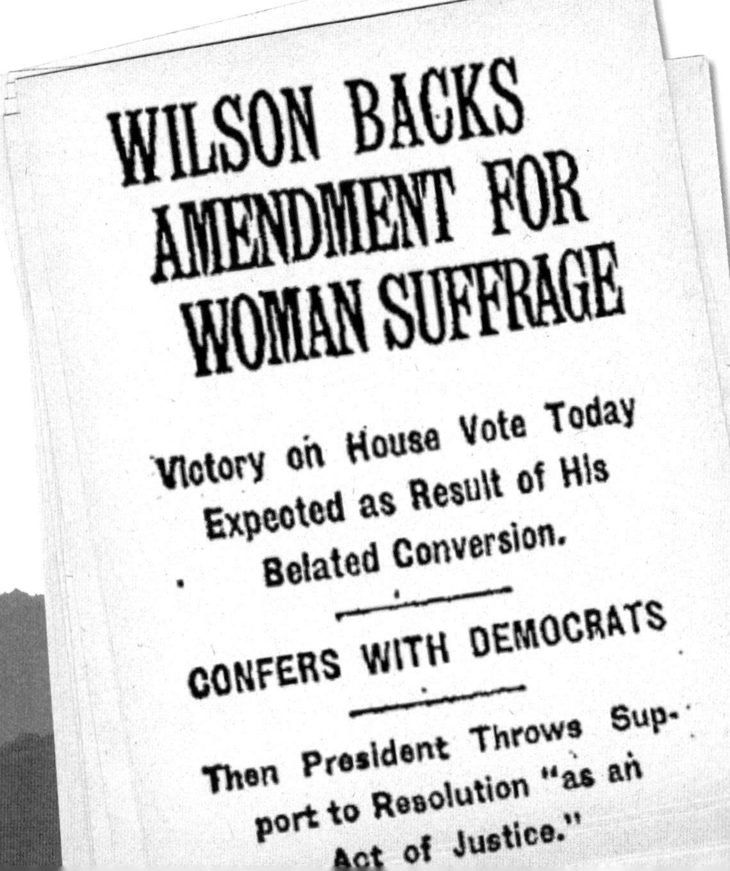

WILSON BACKS AMENDMENT FOR WOMAN SUFFRAGE

Victory on House Vote Today Expected as Result of His Belated Conversion.

CONFERS WITH DEMOCRATS

Then President Throws Support to Resolution "as an Act of Justice."

New York Times, January 10, 1918.

From her Niota farm in Tennessee, Phoebe Burn dashed off a letter to her son. Twenty-four-year-old Harry Burn was a Republican state representative. "Hurrah and vote for Suffrage," she urged him.

The day of the vote, Harry pinned a red rose to his lapel and headed to the state capitol. The red rose signaled that he intended to vote against suffrage.

But Harry had tucked his mother's letter in his pocket. Her words weighed on him. The clerk called Harry's name, and Harry shouted "Aye!"

Another lawmaker also switched his vote and shouted, "Aye!"

With those two votes, the Nineteenth Amendment passed. The federal amendment was signed into law on August 26, 1920.

Women had won the right to vote. It was a victory for America. Women wept and screamed. They waved flags and suffrage banners. They danced and threw yellow flowers.

have to stay at home the
rest of the summer.
The Rockwood crowd is
going to White Cliff Labor
day. Will you be home
by then. Hurrah and
vote for Suffrage and
don't keep them in
doubt. I noticed Chandlers
speech it was ...

After 5 days return to
DEVELOPMENT ASS'N, Inc.
Niota, Tennessee.

NASHVILLE
AUG 17
1920
TENN.

Hon. H. T. Burn
Nashville
Tenn
State Capitol

In a seven-page letter, shown here, Phoebe "Febb" Burn asks her lawmaker son, Harry, to vote for suffrage. Harry does, and later says, "I knew that a mother's advice is always safest for a boy to follow and my mother wanted me to vote for ratification."

VOTES FOR WOMEN

PART FIVE
VICTORY!
VOTES
FOR
WOMEN
VOTES
FOR

NATIONAL

Suffragists raise their arms in celebration as Alice Paul drapes the ratification banner over the balcony at the National Woman's Party headquarters.

AT LAST!

On November 2, 1920, Alice Paul's mother headed to the polls. For the first time, she would vote in a presidential election.

After casting her vote, the mother who pleaded with her daughter to come home from England, who puzzled over her daughter's choices, who worried about her tactics, who didn't approve of her methods, and who asked her to stop annoying the president, wrote in her scrapbook, "Alice at last saw her dream realized."

And so Alice did realize her dream of a federal amendment that guaranteed and protected a woman's right to vote—as did Lucy and the brave women who marched, lobbied, carried picket signs, suffered arrest, and endured prison to win a victory for America.

Here ends the story of Alice Paul and Lucy Burns, who met in a London police station. And yet in so many ways it is the beginning.

AFTERWORD More Work to Be Done

Alice, standing on the right, takes an oath so that she can vote by absentee ballot.

As victory telegrams poured into the NWP headquarters in Washington, DC, someone was missing from the celebrations: Lucy Burns. She had already returned to her much-loved family in Brooklyn, where she likely cast her vote in the November 1920 presidential election. Alice stayed in Washington and voted quietly by absentee ballot. An estimated eight million women voted for the first time.

In all, nearly two thousand suffragists had picketed President Woodrow Wilson. Five hundred women had suffered arrest. One hundred and sixty-eight had endured prison sentences. During a ceremony, the NWP awarded small silver pins to the suffragists who had been imprisoned. The pins were designed as prison doors with a heart-shaped lock.

The executive committee of the National Woman's Party met to set goals for the future. Lucy attended the meeting and then retired, never again to work with Alice or the NWP. After her youngest sister died in childbirth, Lucy devoted herself to a new cause: raising her infant niece. The baby filled Lucy's life and gave her great pleasure. "I have become an impassioned baby minder," Lucy wrote later to her Vassar classmates. In 1966, Lucy died at age 87.

Alice continued to work with the National Woman's Party. The right to vote was a start, but Alice saw more work to be done. She devoted her life to fighting for equal rights for women in all aspects of life. "We shall not be safe," warned Alice in 1923, "until the principle of equal rights is written into the framework of our government."

Up until the day she died in 1977 at age 92, Alice fought for the passage of the Equal Rights Amendment (ERA). The ERA has yet to be added to the Constitution.

Alice Paul, Lucy Burns, and their big idea united women across the country and ended with a victory—the Nineteenth Amendment. But, as Alice warned, the fight for human equality and true democracy isn't over. There's more work to be done.

THE MARCH GOES ON

On January 21, 2017, the Women's March on Washington took place, timed to coincide with the inauguration of President Donald J. Trump. Just as suffragists did in 1913, hundreds of thousands of women and their allies surged down Pennsylvania Avenue, protesting the new president's conduct and his policies. Millions more marched in cities across the United States and around the world, on all seven continents. Here, demonstrators are shown gathered at the National Mall. In the distance, behind the Washington Monument, the Lincoln Memorial can be seen.

BEFORE ALICE MET LUCY

A Timeline of Significant Suffrage Events in the United States

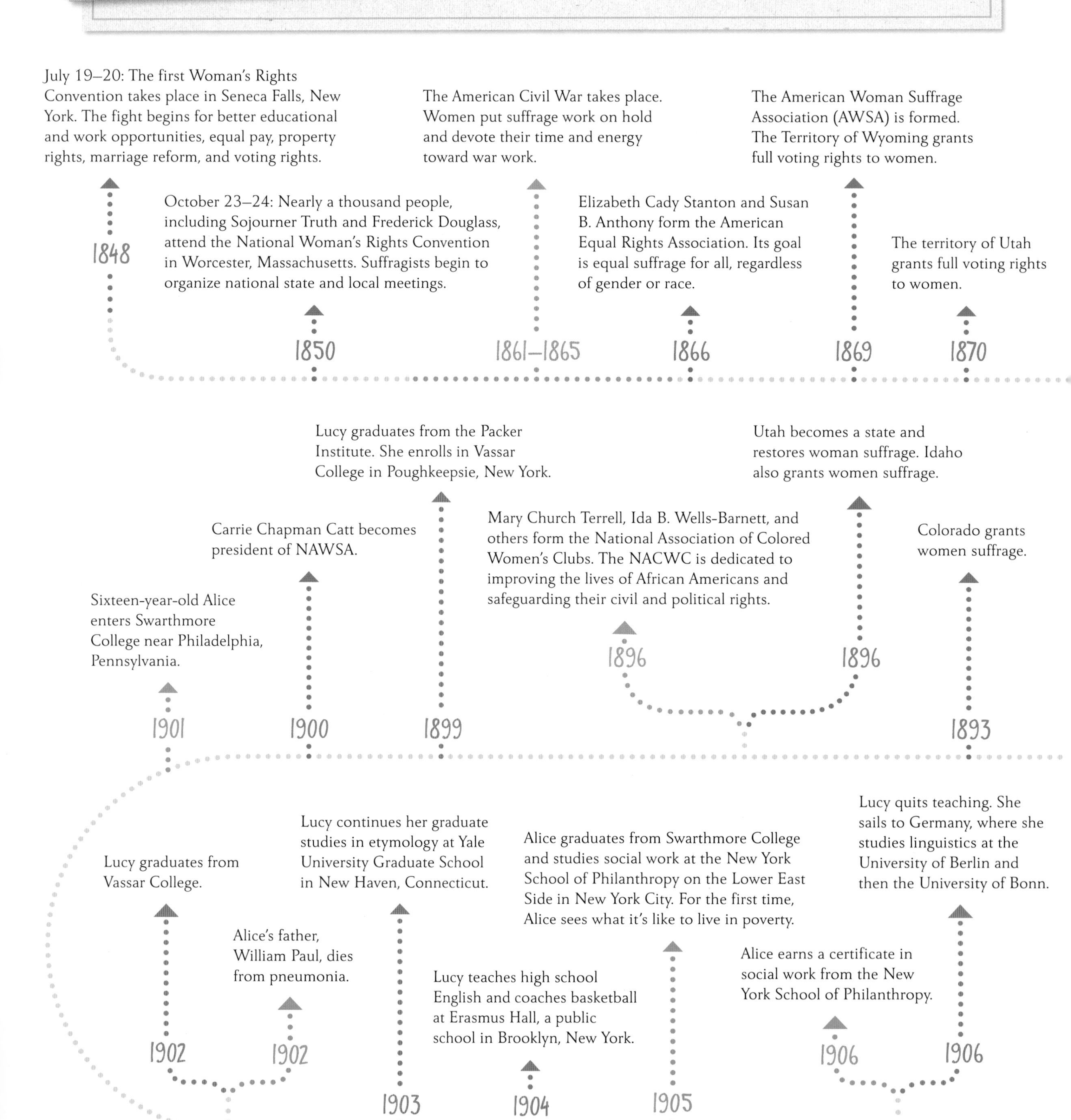

- Blue=US or UK events
- Purple=Suffrage events
- Green= Alice events
- Red=Lucy events

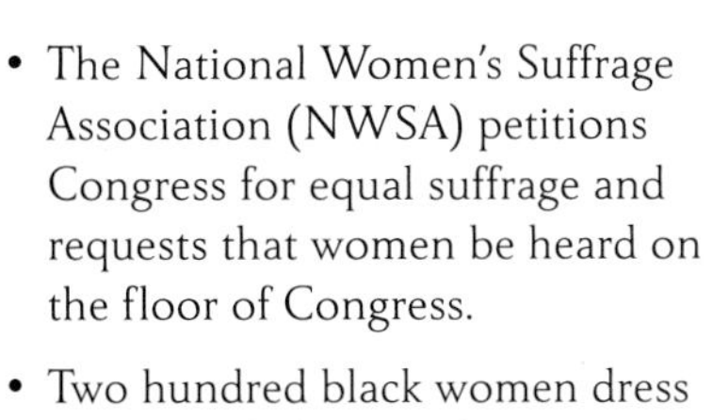

1871

- The National Women's Suffrage Association (NWSA) petitions Congress for equal suffrage and requests that women be heard on the floor of Congress.
- Two hundred black women dress in men's clothing and vote in Johnson County, North Carolina.

1872

Susan B. Anthony is arrested and fined $100 for voting. Elsewhere, fifteen women are arrested for voting. Sojourner Truth is turned away at a polling booth in Battle Creek, Michigan.

1876

At the July 4th Centennial Program at Independence Hall in Philadelphia, Susan B. Anthony and other NWSA leaders pass out flyers titled "The Declaration of the Rights of Women of the United States." Ninety-four black women ask to add their names to the Declaration. The NWSA does not add their names.

1878

A Woman Suffrage Amendment is proposed and later defeated in the US Congress.

1879

July 28: Lucy Burns is born in Brooklyn Heights, New York, to Edward and Ann Burns. Lucy has three older sisters and will be the fourth of eight children.

1883

The territory of Washington grants full voting rights to women.

1885

January 11: Alice Stokes Paul is born to William and Tacie Stokes Paul in Mt. Laurel, New Jersey. Alice will have two younger brothers and a sister.

1887

Congress revokes the right of women to vote in Utah.

1890

Wyoming is admitted as a state to the Union.

1890

Lucy Burns attends the all-girls Packer Collegiate Institute.

1890

NWSA and AWSA merge, forming the National American Woman Suffrage Association (NAWSA).

1891

Alice attends the Moorestown Friends School in Moorestown, New Jersey.

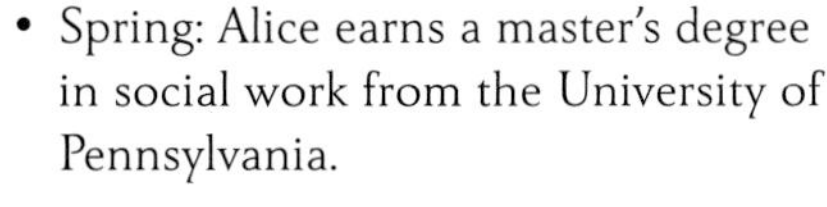

1907

- Spring: Alice earns a master's degree in social work from the University of Pennsylvania.
- Summer: Alice moves to Berlin, Germany, and studies at the University of Bonn.
- Fall: Alice studies at Woodbrooke Study Center in Birmingham, England, and works at a settlement house.
- December: Alice attends her first suffrage event, sponsored by the Women's Social and Political Union (WSPU).

1908

- June 21: Alice attends a large suffrage rally in London. The next month Alice marches in two parades and attends weekly meetings.
- Fall: Alice enrolls in the London School of Economics.

1909

June 29: Alice and Lucy line up at Caxton Hall in London. They to join two hundred women in a protest march to Parliament.

1909

- Lucy enrolls in the doctoral program at Oxford University in London, England, to study linguistics.
- After attending a suffrage meeting, Lucy quits Oxford and joins the Woman's Social and Political Union (WSPU).

1909

Alice sells newspapers on street corners for the suffrage cause.

SOURCES & NOTES

For anyone wishing to dive deeper into the story of Alice Paul, Lucy Burns, and the brave women who won the vote, I recommend Mary Walton's *A Woman's Crusade: Alice Paul and the Battle for the Ballot* (New York: St. Martin's Griffin, 2016) and J. D. Zahniser and Amelia Fry's *Alice Paul: Claiming Power* (New York: Oxford University Press, 2014).

Alice's personality and passion for the suffrage cause shine in her letters to her long-suffering mother, Tacie Paul. The Alice Paul Papers are housed at the Schlesinger Library, Harvard University, Cambridge, Massachusetts, and available online, https://hollisarchives.lib.harvard.edu/repositories/8/resources/5012. And don't miss hearing Alice herself in a conversation with Amelia Fry, at www.alicepaul.org/audio-interview/.

Below you'll find full citations for sources and attributions for instances of direct quotes, indirect quotes, paraphrased quotes, or a person's thoughts or feelings, as well as notes to extend or deepen a discussion. Enjoy! I did.

Page 7. *Wear your heaviest . . . protect your body*: Alice Paul, "Conversations with Alice Paul: Woman Suffrage and the Equal Rights Amendment," interview by Amelia R. Fry, 48–49. Transcript available at www.alicepaul.org/audio-interview/

Page 8. "La Marseillaise": Estelle Sylvia Pankhurst, *The Suffragette: the history of the women's militant suffrage movement, 1905–1910* (New York: Sturgis & Walton Co., 1911), 384. To the tune of the French anthem, British suffragettes wrote the "Women's Marseillaise." The 1908 protest song begins with the words "Arise! Ye daughters of a land/That vaunts its liberty!/May restless rulers understand/That women must be free/That women *will* be free."

Page 8. *Eyes forward!*: *New York Times*, May 4, 1913, 1.

Page 10. *Votes for Women!* and *Shame! Shame!*: Alice Paul, letters to "Mamma," n.d. July 1909, MC 399, Identifier 29, Alice Paul papers.

Page 11. *"We have come here"*: Pankhurst, *The Suffragette*, 385; Paul, *Conversations*, 48; Paul, letters to "Mamma," n.d. July 1909.

Page 11. *"The Prime Minister . . . regrets"*: Pankhurst, *The Suffragette*, 385.

Page 12. *"Deeds Not Words"*: Paula Bartley, *Emmeline Pankhurst* (London and New York: Routledge, 2012), 116.

Page 13. *The crowd shouted*: Paul, letters to "Mamma," n.d. July 1909.

Page 15. *"Dear Mamma . . . one awful nightmare"*: Paul, letters to "Mamma," n.d. July 1909.

Page 15. *But Alice wasn't ready*: Paul, letters to "Mamma," July 10, 1909.

Page 16. *"We had thrilling times"*: Paul, letters to "Mamma," July 10, 1909. See Alice's letters, July 10 through October 27, 1909, for the quotes and descriptions included here and for her gleeful accounts of her escapades to her much-worried mother. Later, Alice doesn't recall—and then denies—that she climbed onto the St. Andrew Halls roof (see Paul, *Conversations*, xiv, 53). The incident, however, is reported in the *Glasgow Herald*, August 21, 1909, 8.

In her letters home, Alice explains that suffragettes used hunger strikes as a means of nonviolent resistance to a government that treated them as criminals and not as political prisoners exercising their right to petition the government.

Page 16. *"I cannot understand"*: *New York Times*, November 13, 1909, 6. It seems hard to believe that Alice puzzled her mother. As Quakers, Alice and her family did not support violence or war. They believed people are equal and should work to improve society. Some Quakers, including Alice's own ancestors, went to prison when they stood up for their beliefs.

Page 17. *"How can you dine"*: *New York Times*, November 12, 1909, 1.

Page 17. *"Votes for Women!"*: Paul, *Conversations*, 56; *New York Times*, January 21, 1910, 18; *Philadelphia Inquirer*, January 21, 1910, 1, 7.

Page 18. *This is called a force-feeding*: *Philadelphia Tribune*, January 22, 1910, 1; *New York Times*, December 10, 1909, 1. Today, the American Medical Association and the Red Cross condemn force-feeding a prisoner as a form of torture. In later life, Alice refused to talk about the forced feedings, explaining that she had "vanquished" the past. Alice Paul, "I Was Arrested, Of Course," Interview by Robert Gallagher. *American Heritage*, February 1974, Vol. 25, Issue 2. www.americanheritage.com/alice-paul-i-was-arrested-course.

Page 19. *"I hope I will never"*: Paul, letters to "Mamma," December 27, 1909.

Page 22. *"You must resort . . . over there"*: *Philadelphia Inquirer*, January 21, 1910, 1, 7.

Page 23. *Alice grew excited*: Caroline Katzenstein, Lifting the Curtain (Philadelphia: Dorrance & Company, 1955), 44.

Page 25. *Alice and Lucy visited*: Paul, *Conversations*, 63.

Page 26. *"hysterical"*: William Howard Taft, "Votes for Women," *The Saturday Evening Post*, September 11, 1919, 5. "On the whole," wrote Taft, "it is fair to say that the immediate enfranchisement of women will increase the proportion of the hysterical element of the electorate to such a degree that it will be injurious to the public welfare."

Page 26. *"a fundamental necessity"*: Woodrow Wilson, *The New Freedom: A Call for the Emancipation of the Generous Energies of a People* (Garden City, New York: Doubleday, Page & Co., 1921), 294.

Page 26. *It's time to take*: Paul, *Conversations*, 63–65.

Page 27. *Alice predicted one year*: Paul, *American Heritage*. Here, Alice explains, "When you're young, when you've never done anything very much on your own, you imagine that it won't be so hard."

Page 28. *The Treasury will not contribute*: Paul, *Conversations*, 65, 72–74; Paul, *American Heritage*.

Page 30. *This woman wanted . . . No other day would do*: Paul, *Conversations*, 72–73; *Hearings*, 128–136. Later, Alice denied difficulty in obtaining the permit (see Paul, *American Heritage*.)

Page 30. *You're asking for trouble, "riff-raff,"* and *"roughscuff"*: United States. "Suffrage Parade. Hearings before a Subcommittee of the Committee on the District of Columbia, United States Senate, Sixty-third Congress, Special Session of the Senate, V.1.," HathiTrust, Accessed October 19, 2019. https://babel.hathitrust.org/cgi/pt?id=hvd.rslfb8&view=1up&seq=5, 131–132.

Page 31. *"right to the avenue"* . . . Sylvester caved: Paul, *Conversations,* 72–73; *Washington Post,* January 10, 1913, 2.

Page 33. *A Piegan Blackfoot woman*: *Brooklyn Daily Eagle,* March 3, 1913, 8.

Page 34. *In mid-January, a schoolteacher*: Paul, *Conversations,* 133–134; Sidney Roderick Bland, *Techniques of Persuasion: The National Woman's Party and Woman Suffrage, 1913–1919,* PhD diss., George Washington University, 1972, 54–55; Walton, *A Woman's Crusade,* 63–65; and Mary Walton, "The Day the Deltas Marched into History," *Washington Post,* March 01, 2013. Accessed April 08, 2019. https://www.washingtonpost.com/opinions/the-day-the-deltas-marched-into-history/2013/03/01/eabbf130-811d-11e2-b99e-6baf4ebe42df_story.html

Page 34. *But when black women*: *The Crisis,* Vol. 5, No. 6 (April 1913), 42–43.

Page 34. *Alice offered a compromise*: Paul, *Conversations,* 133–134; Bland, *Techniques of Persuasion,* 53; Walton, *A Woman's Crusade,* 64. Alice insisted that she, as a Quaker, believed in equality. From her remarks in *Conversations,* however, Alice's failure to act seems to stem from her fear that she'd lose the "many, many, many splendid supporters" who refused to march with black women.

Page 35. *"We do not wish"*: Zahniser and Fry, *Alice Paul: Claiming Power,* 140–141; Walton, "The Day the Deltas Marched."

Page 35. *"I shall not march"*: *Chicago Daily Tribune,* March 4, 1913, 3.

Page 35. *"The suffrage movement stands"* . . . *Let black women*: Walton, *A Woman's Crusade,* 64; Bland, *Techniques of Persuasion,* 55.

Page 37. *"This is a woman's movement"*: *Washington Post,* February 22, 1913, 1.

Page 37. *Anna Howard Shaw refused . . . parade route*: Walton, *A Woman's Crusade,* 65–67.

Page 37. *Twice, Alice asked Sylvester . . . Boy Scout*: Paul, *Conversations,* 72–73; *Hearings,* 128–136, 211. See also "What the Boy Scouts Did at the Inauguration," *Boy's Life,* April 1913, 2–4.

Page 39. *"If the Illinois women"*: *Chicago Daily Tribune,* March 4, 1913, 3.

Page 45. *"I am doing it"*: *Chicago Daily Tribune,* March 4, 1913, 3.

Page 48. *Many smelled like the seedy* . . . *"sidewalk falls through"*: *Chicago Daily Tribune,* March 7, 1913, 1; *New York Times,* March 5, 1913, 8; *Hearings,* 7, 28, 31–32, 35, 111, 128–143, 461.

Page 49. *"Girls, get out your hat pins"*: *Hearings,* 456.

Page 54. *"Somebody has to make:"* as quoted in Walton, *A Woman's Crusade,* 126.

Page 54. *Boycott! Boycott Democrats!*: Paul, *Conversations,* 129; Zahniser and Fry, 194.

Page 54. *Call off the boycott*: Paul, *Conversations,* 326; Zahniser and Fry, 229–230

Page 57. *Just sit on the stage*: Paul, *Conversations,* 172; Walton, *A Woman's Crusade,* 141. Inez suffered from pernicious anemia and was too weak to undergo surgery for infected tonsils.

Page 57. *"president wilson how long"*: Stevens, 48.

Page 58. *"Why do you oppose"*: *Suffragist,* July 8, 1917; Zahniser and Fry, 244.

Page 59. *"Puerto Rico," "Suffragists,"* and *"We feel we did our duty"*: *Boston Post,* December 6, 1916, 1, 3; *Philadelphia Inquirer,* December 6, 1916, 1, 5; *Gazette Times* (Pittsburgh, Pennsylvania), December 6, 1916, 1, 3; *Warren Evening Times* (Pennsylvania), Dec. 6, 1916, 1.

Page 60. *"bad manners and mad banners"*: *Washington Post,* April 23, 1917, 8.

Page 60. *"childish"*: as quoted in Walton, *A Woman's Crusade,* 154.

Page 60. *"Silly women," "crazy,"* and *"pathological"*: Doris Stevens, *Jailed for Freedom* (New York: Boni and Liveright, Inc., 1920), 64.

Page 61. *"Dear Alice, I wish"*: as quoted in Walton, *A Woman's Crusade,* 150.

Page 62. *"safe for democracy"*: Wilson, "Joint Address to Congress Leading to a Declaration of War Against Germany (1917)," https://www.ourdocuments.gov/ doc.php?flash=false&doc= 61&page=transcript. See also Paul, *Conversations,* 175–176. Alice notes that one woman —Jeannette Rankin— voted against the war. "We told her we thought it would be a tragedy for the first woman ever in Congress to vote for war," said Paul. "That the one thing that seemed to us so clear was that the women were the peace-loving half of the world and that by giving power to women we would diminish the possibilities of war."

Page 63. *We, the women of America*: Stevens 92.

Page 63. *"Treason!" "Shame!"* . . . *"Come on, boys"*: *New York Times,* June 21, 1917, 1, 2.

Page 64. *Guilty! Pay a twenty-five dollar*: *The Suffragist,* July 21, 1917, 7.

Page 64. *"It will merely be"*: as quoted in Walton, *A Woman's Crusade,* 192.

Page 65. *"Shut up there, you!"*: as quoted in Walton, *A Woman's Crusade,* 200.

Page 66. *"an act of right and justice"*: *New York Times,* January 10, 1918, 1.

Page 67. *"Hurrah and vote for suffrage"*: Phoebe Burn, Harry T. Burn Papers, C. M. McClung Historical Collection, Knox County Public Library System, Knoxville, Tennessee.

Page 71. *"Alice at last saw her dream realized"*: Tacie Paul's Scrapbook, Alice Paul Papers, MC 399, Identifier 211.

Page 72. *"I have become"*: Lucy Burns, Eighteenth Annual Bulletin (1931), Vassar University Library Special Collections, 11.

Page 72. *"We shall not be safe"*: https://www.equalrightsamendment.org/history. Has your state ratified the ERA? Find out here: https://www.equalrightsamendment.org/era-ratification-map

In Illinois, voters from Chicago and Cicero used this wooden box to cast their ballots on the woman suffrage question on April 9, 1912. Illinois would grant women the right to vote on June 12, 1913.

FURTHER READING FOR THE YOUNG ACTIVIST

What Young People Have Done and Can Do

Marching for Freedom: Walk Together, Children, and Don't You Grow Weary by Elizabeth Partridge

Notorious RBG: The Life and Times of Ruth Bader Ginsburg, Young Reader's Edition, by Irin Carmon and Shana Knizhnik

Shaking Things Up: 14 Young Women Who Changed the World by Susan Hood, illustrated by Selina Alko, Sophie Blackall, Lisa Brown, Hadley Hooper, Emily Winfield Martin, Oge Mora, Julie Morstad, Sara Palacios, LeUyen Pham, Erin Robinson, Isabel Roxas, Shadra Strickland, Melissa Sweet

Shall Not Be Denied: Women Fight for the Vote, the Official Companion to the Library of Congress Exhibition, with a foreword by Carla D. Hayden

We Were There, Too! Young People in U.S. History by Phillip Hoose

You Are Mighty: A Guide to Changing the World by Caroline Paul, illustrated by Lauren Tamaki

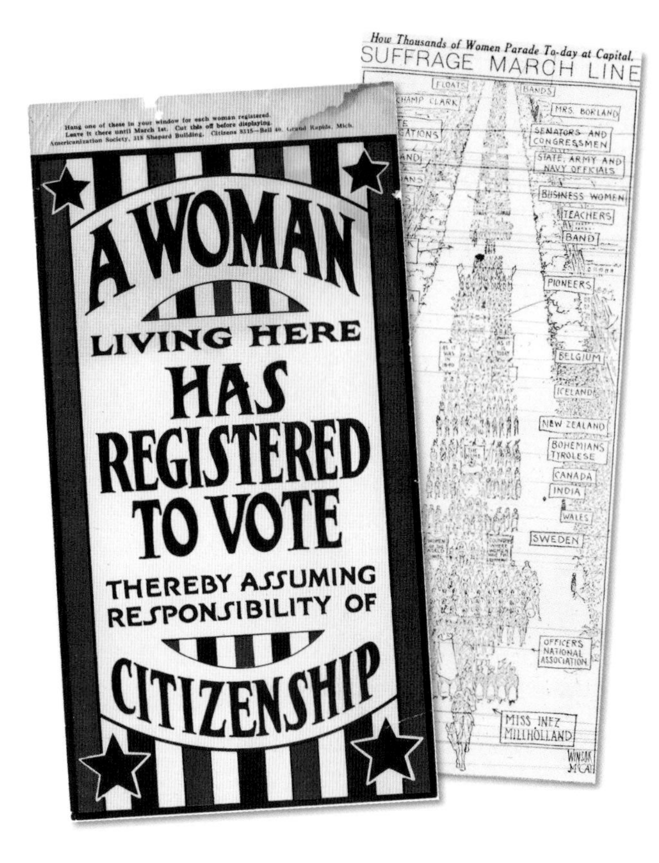

IMAGE CREDITS

A hearty thanks goes to the following archives and institutions, and their specialists, for allowing me to obtain images and granting me permission for their use.

Chung W. Lee/*The New York Times*/Redux: Page 73

Chicago Daily Tribune, March 5, 1913, 3: page 45 (top)

Chicago Historical Society: page 77

freeUSandworldmaps.com: page 16

Getty: page 19

Harry T. Burn Papers, C. M. McClung Historical Collection, Knox County Public Library System, Knoxville, TN: page 67

Library of Congress: pages 7 (left, right), 22, 26 (top, middle, bottom), 28 (top), 28 (middle), 29 (middle left, bottom), 30, 32 (top left, middle, bottom left, bottom middle, bottom right), 33 (top left, right, bottom left, bottom right), 35, 36 (top, middle, bottom), 37 (top left, top right), 44 (top, middle, bottom), 45 (middle, bottom), 46–47, 50–51, 54 (top, bottom), 55 (top, bottom), 56–57, 57 (top), 60–61, 64 (left), 65, 70–71, 72, 78 (top right), 80

National Museum of American History, Smithsonian Institution: pages 29 (middle right), 32 (button), 33 (buttons), 42–43, 44 (button), 45 (buttons), 72 (pin), 77 (bottom left), 78 (top left), 79 (button)

Sewall-Belmont House & Museum, National Woman's Party Photograph Collection: pages 32 (top right), 55 (middle), 64 (bottom right)

Special Collections Research Center, Temple University Libraries, Philadelphia PA: page 62

The Women's Library Collection, LSE Library, London UK: page 15

Trinity Mirror/Mirropix/Alamy: page 12

University of Washington Libraries, Special Collections: page 33 (bottom middle)

The images on pages 29 (top), 37 (button), and 79 come from my personal collection.

Endpaper images come from the Alice Paul Papers, courtesy of the Schlesinger Library, Harvard University, Cambridge, Massachusetts.

ACKNOWLEDGMENTS

I'm indebted to many people for their insights, encouragement, services, hard work, and dedication: my ever-patient, ever-imaginative, ever-hardworking editor Jill Davis and her equally dedicated team, including Honee Jang, Chelsea C. Donaldson, Jessica Berg, and Gwen Morton; my agent extraordinaire, Ginger Knowlton; Nancy Cummings and Elizabeth Partridge for swooping in; my history-lovin' husband, Joe; and above all, the brave women who have marched and continue to march for full equality for all, in all aspects of life.

A heartfelt thanks also goes to Dana Smith and Nelson Steffy, who shepherded family memorabilia into my hands. In a dusty box, they found a framed photograph that sent me hunting through historical records for an answer to the question: Did my grandmother Mercedes Simmons Campbell leave her Scranton, Pennsylvania, home on November 2, 1920, and become one of the estimated eight million women who voted for the first time in a presidential election?

Yes, indeed, the historical record shows that Mercedes did vote.

Mercedes Simmons Campbell

INDEX

Alpha Kappa Alpha, 34, 39
American Civil War, 74
American Equal Rights Association, 74
American ideals 45, 46–47, 46–47 (photo)
Charity, Justice, Plenty, Liberty, Peace, Hope, 46, 46–47 (photo)
American Woman Suffrage Association (AWSA), 74
Anthony, Susan B., 74
anti-suffrage, 36–37
headquarters, 37 (photo)
arrests, 5, 12–13, 16, 64–65, 72, 74
Arizona, 25
Asquith, Herbert Henry, 11, 17
prime minister, 6

black women, 34–35, 39, 44, 74–75
activism and, 34–35, 44, 74-75
clubs, 34, 35, 35 (photo), 74
professionals, 35
racial discrimination and, 39, 44, 75, 77
Bly, Nellie, 32 (photo), 33
boycotts, 54–56
Boy Scouts, 36 (photo), 37, 51
Brown, Amelia, 17
Burn, Harry T., 67
Burn, Phoebe "Febb," 67, 67 (photo)
Burns, Lucy (7) photo, 17, 25, 32 (photo)
Alice Paul and, 7, 13, 14, 15, 22–23, 26–27, 57, 71
arrests of, 13, 16, 64, 65
boycotts and, 55, 55 (photo)
early life, 74–75
family, 13, 24, 72, 74–75
hunger strike and, 16, 65
National Woman's Party and, 56
Occoquan workhouse, 64, 65, 65 (photo)
parade and, 28, 32–33, 38, 33, 39, 49, 51
pickets and, 63
Woodrow Wilson and, 58, 59
Burroughs, Nannie Helen, 35 (photo)

California, 25
Cannon Row Police Station, 5
Catt, Carrie Chapman, 54, 60, 60 (photo), 74
Churchill, Winston, 16, 17
Clifford, Carrie Williams, 34
Colorado, 25

"Deeds Not Words," 12
Delta Sigma Theta, 34, 39
Democrats, 26, 53, 54, 55, 66
democracy, 62, 63
Douglass, Frederick, 74

Equal Rights Amendment (ERA), 72

federal amendment, 56, 60, 66
floats, 33, 38, 41, 44, 45,
force-feeding, 18, 65, 76

Great Britain, 6, 16 (map)
Great Demand, 29, 41
Great War, 62, 66, 77
Guildhall, 17

hecklers, 10, 48–49, 58–59
hikers, 36, 36 (photo), 39
Hobson, Richmond P., 33, 33 (photo)
Holloway Prison, 17, 18, 19 (photo)
Holme, Vera "Jack", 15 (photo)
Homemakers Association, 44, 44 (photo)
Howard University, 34
hunger strikes, 16, 18, 22, 65, 76

Idaho, 25
Illinois, 39, 45

Jones, Rosalie "General," 36 (photo), 39

Kansas, 25
Keller, Helen, 32 (photo), 33

MacKaye, Hazel, 29 (photo)
"Mamma" (Tacie Paul), 15, 16, 19, 21, 61, 64, 73
"La Marseillaise," 8, 57, 76
mice, 37
Milholland, Inez, 29 (photo), 41, 44, 51, 57
Mist, Dawn, 33, 33 (photo)
mobs, 49, 50–51, 50–51 (photo), 63
Montana, 25
Morey, Katharine, 63, 64
Mullowney, Alexander R., 64

National American Woman Suffrage Association (NAWSA), 22, 28, 34, 35, 44 (photo), 54, 56
and discrimination, 34
National Association of Colored Women's Clubs (NACWC), 34, 35, 74
National Woman's Party (NWP), 56, 59, 60–61, 66, 72
Nineteenth Amendment, 67, 72
Noyes, Florence Fleming, 33 (photo), 33

Occoquan Workhouse, 64, 65, 65 (photo), 72
Oregon, 25

pageant, 29, 29 (photo), 33, 33 (photo), 45, 45 (photo), 46–47, 46–47 (photo)
Pankhurst, Emmeline, 11–12, 12 (photo), 15, 15 (photo)
parade, 27–31, 32–33, 32–33 (photos), 34–35, 36–37, 36–37 (photos), 38–39, 41, 42–43 (photo), 44–45, 44–45 (photos), 46–47, 46–47 (photo), 50–51 (photo), 51
parade route, 29, 32 (map), 44–45
Paul, Alice, 7, 7 (photo), 15, 17, 22, 22 (photo), 24–25, 76, 77
and anti-suffragists, 37
arrests and imprisonment, 13, 16, 18–19, 64 (photo), 64–64
and chalk, 24
and ERA, 72
and Lucy Burns, 7, 12, 14, 23–23, 26–27,
hunger strikes, 16, 18–19, 22
family, 21
forced feeding, 18, 19, 65, 76,
letters to Mamma, 15, 16, 19, 64
letter from Mamma, 61
and mobs, 49, 51
parade planning, 28–29, 32–33
and purple hat, 22, 39
and Richard H. Sylvester, 30–31, 37
racial discrimination, 34–35
and ratification banner, 66, 70–71 (photo)
Woodrow Wilson and, 51, 52, 56
voting, 72
Paul, Parry, 21
Paul, Tacie (Mamma), 15, 16, 19, 21, 61, 64, 73
Pennsylvania Avenue, 27, 30, 31, 41, 42–43 (photo), 48–49, 73
Philadelphia, Pennsylvania, 21, 22, 23
pickets, 60–61, 60–61 (photo), 62,
police, 11, 12, 12 (photo), 13, 17, 30–31, 37, 49, 51
police brutality, 5, 13

Quander, Nellie May, 20–21 34–35, 39

racial discrimination, 35–35, 39, 75
Rankin, Jeannete, 77
Reicher, Hedwig, 45
as Columbia, 45 (photo), 46
riot, 12–13, 48–49, 50–51

Shaw, Anna Howard, 28, 28 (photo), 37, 54
Stanton, Elizabeth Cady, 74
suffragettes, 6, 10–11, 14, 15, 17, 22, 24, 28, 76
difference between suffragettes and suffragists, 11, 28
suffragists, 11, 28, 36, 44, 55, 56, 57, 59, 62, 66, 72, 74
suffrage headquarters 28, 28 (photo), 31, 37, 56, 64 (photo), 70–71 (photo), 72
Sylvester, Richard H., 30 (photo), 30–31, 37, 48

Taft, William Howard, 26, 26 (photo), 76
Terrell, Mary Church, 34–35, 39, 60, 74
Timms, Walter, 63
Truth, Sojourner, 74, 75

Utah, 25

Vale, Margaret, 32 (photo), 33
Woodrow Wilson and, 33
Vernon, Mabel, 55, 55 (photo), 58–59, 60

Washington, 25
Washington, DC, 29 (map)
Wells-Barnett, Ida B., 34–35, 45, 45 (photo)
Whittaker, Raymond, 65
Wilson, Woodrow, 26, 26 (photo), 33, 53, 54, 56, 56 (photo), 58–62, 62 (photo), 63, 66, 72
Woman's National Baptist Convention, 35 (photo)
Woman's March on Washington, 73
Women's Social and Political Union (WSPU), 75
Wyoming, 25

National Woman's Party

NATIONAL HEADQUARTERS, ~~LAFAYETTE SQUARE~~ 25 First st. N. E.
WASHINGTON, D. C.

July 5 - 1921

Dear Mother -

Thank thee for the $50 which I am glad to have. I cannot go to Squirrel Inn as I am studying law and cannot get away. I am taking double work by going to both George Washington University law school and the Washington College of Law. One place has classes in the evening and one has classes in the day. By doing this I can graduate next summer, I think - This is what I am trying to do.

Enclosed are photographs showing the permanent Headquarters that we are purchasing. Mrs Belmont has just sent us a cheque for $51,500 to cover the cost of one of the houses in the group of three which we are endeavoring